MR. RUSH

by Roger Hargreaves

Mr Rush was the fastest thing on two legs.

He used to rush hither and thither, and thither and hither, and back again, all the time.

And, of course, he was always in such a rush that he never ever finished anything properly.

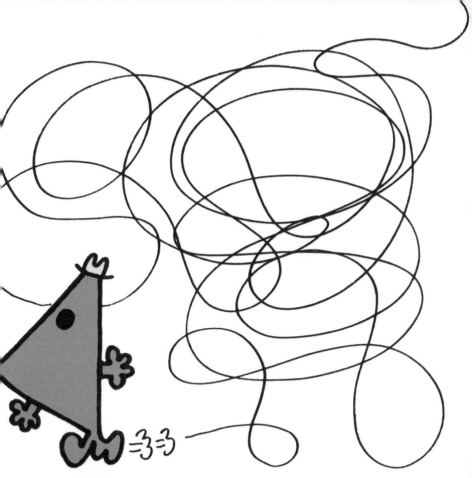

One morning he woke up with a jump.

He'd only had time for three hours' sleep because he'd been rushing about for so long the day before.

"Oh dear," he cried, leaping out of bed. "I'm late!"

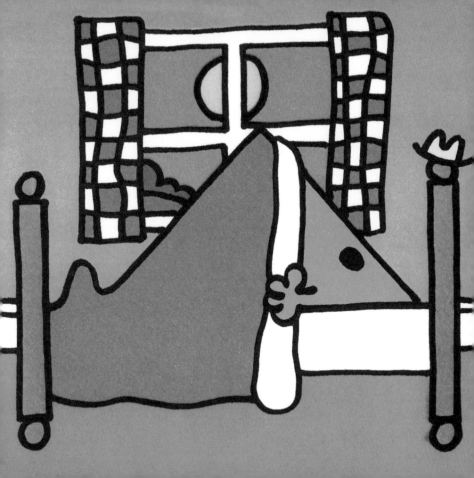

And he rushed into his bathroom, and washed (not very well as he was in such a hurry) and cleaned one tooth, and rushed downstairs – three at a time.

Mr Rush had a boiled egg and toast and a cup of tea for breakfast.

He boiled the egg for five seconds, and it tasted awful.

He toasted the bread for one second, and so it wasn't brown at all.

And, as he couldn't bear to wait for the kettle to boil, he made his tea with cold water.

Ugh!

What a horrid breakfast.

And, of course, he was in such a rush he only ate half of it.

Rush. Rush. Rush.

Silly fellow!

After his half a breakfast he rushed off again.

Out of his front door (leaving it open), down his garden path, out of his garden gate (leaving it open too), and off down the lane.

He passed Mr Happy.

"Hello," called Mr Happy. "Good morning, Mr Rush. Where are you off to?"

"Can't stop," cried Mr Rush. "I'm in much too much of a hurry!"

"I can see that," thought Mr Happy to himself as he watched Mr Rush disappear into the distance. "I wonder where he's going?"

Where Mr Rush was going was nowhere.

Fast!

As usual.

Mr Rush rushed around all morning, and then rushed home and had a quick bite to eat (a sandwich without bread), and then rushed off again.

And rushed around all afternoon!

That evening, he was reading a magazine (he never had time to read a book) when he saw an advertisement for a holiday.

"Ooo," he said. "I'd like that. Haven't had a holiday for ages."

But then his face fell.

"I can't go on holiday," he thought, "because I don't have any money."

And then he thought again.

And his face rose.

"I know," he thought, "I'll get a job."

And so, the following morning, he rushed off and got a job.

With a farmer.

Milking cows!

But of course he wasn't any good at that because, if there's one thing a cow can't stand, it's being rushed.

Especially when it's being milked!

So, Mr Rush rushed off and got himself another job.

Driving a bus!

But of course he wasn't any good at that because he was always in such a rush he never stopped at any of the bus stops!

And, if there's one thing people waiting at a bus stop don't like, it's when the bus doesn't stop for them.

So, Mr Rush rushed off and got himself another job.

As a waiter in a hotel!

But of course he wasn't any good at that because, no sooner had he served people a meal, and they'd taken one bite, than he whisked the plate away from under their noses.

And, if there's one thing hungry people can't stand, its having food whisked away from them.

Poor Mr Rush.

No job.

No money!

"Oh dear," he sighed to himself. "I'm never going to be able to go on holiday."

He looked very glum and gloomy.

But then an idea struck him.

An idea for a job for someone who rushes around all the time.

An ideal job for someone who was the fastest thing on two legs.

Do you know what that job was?

Would you like to know what that job was?

Postman!

Delivering express letters.

Mr Rush was so good at it, he delivered twice as many letters in half the time any postman had ever done it before.

Soon he had saved enough money for that holiday of his.

And so, the very next week, there was Mr Rush sitting on a beach in the hot sunshine under a palm tree on holiday.

"This is the life," he grinned.

And rushed off for a swim.

His fifteenth that day!

And then it was breakfast time!